Spring Waters
Gathering Places

Published by The Watercourse

Written by Sandra Chisholm DeYonge,
Associate Director The Watercourse

With support from The Watercourse Staff
Dennis Nelson, Stephanie Ouren,
Bonnie Sachatello-Sawyer, Chandra Morris,
Linda Hveem, Gary Cook, John Etgen,
Kristen Limb, Sally Unser

Illustrated by Peter Grosshauser
Designed by Bryan Knaff

WATERCOURSE

International
W E T
Water Education for Teachers

THE Perrier GROUP

DEER PARK	Zephyrhills	ICE MOUNTAIN
Ozarka	Poland Spring	Perrier
CALISTOGA	ARROWHEAD	S.PELLEGRINO

SPRING WATERS, GATHERING PLACES

The goal of The Watercourse is to promote and facilitate public understanding of atmospheric, surface, and ground water resources, and related management issues through publications, instruction, and networking. Project WET (Water Education for Teachers) is a program of The Watercourse.

Printed by Creasey Printing Services

The story "Native Americans: The Cheyenne" is adapted from the Cheyenne myth titled "The Old Woman of the Spring." It is found in the book *American Indian Myths and Legends* by Richard Erdoes and Alfonso Ortiz, copyright 1984 by Richard Erdoes and Alfonso Ortiz. The story is reprinted by permission of Pantheon Books, a division of Random House, Inc.

Published by The Watercourse
201 Culbertson Hall
Montana State University
Bozeman, Montana 59717-0570
www.projectwet.org
(406) 994-5392

DeYonge, Sandra Chisholm
  Spring Waters, Gathering Places: Sandra Chisholm DeYonge;
 Illustrated by Peter Grosshauser
 Designed by Bryan Knaff
 Summary: Early people thought that springs were a gift from the earth. Beautifully illustrated stories and myths chronicle the use of spring waters through time. Games and investigations lead readers to an understanding of ground water, springs, and the importance of healthy water for healthy people everywhere.

ISBN 1-888631-05-8

Spring Waters
Gathering Places

Spring water is a miracle of nature, one we want to share with you and celebrate with this book. At the Perrier Group, we are committed to educating young people about water: its power and beauty, and the importance of using it wisely. Our springs are our lifeblood. Through sound science, we harvest only what nature can safely replenish. Stewardship of the natural resources we own is our top priority and it is a legacy we want to pass on to others.

Kim Jeffery
President and CEO
Perrier Group of America

Table of Contents

Coyote

Long before humans discovered springs, only plants and other animals used them. In fact, many of the trails to water that animals traveled were later followed by people. Some animals like coyotes even knew to dig wells when pools and seeps dried up during times of drought. These places are called "coyote wells." This story shows how animals—specifically, a family of coyotes—depended on spring waters for survival.

A restlessness came over the female coyote. Since sunrise she had been hunting with her mate. And although the earth echoed with the sounds of prey, she had not moused with her usual success.

She felt light and heavy at the same time; tired, but excited. As soon as she lay down, she felt the urge to move again. She left her mate. Starting from a walk, she changed smoothly to a steady trot, and finally settled into an easy lope. Her four legs pumped rhythmically beneath her. Her muscles rippled under the coarse gray fur and her bushy, black-tipped tail streamed behind her.

Following her instincts, she traveled for several miles. The land that had been hard and sometimes rocky beneath her feet gradually became soft, almost spongy. She moved through tall reeds, disturbing them no more than a gentle breeze. Finally, she stood at the edge of a clear pool. She drank until she was satisfied.

As she lifted her head, the clear water streamed from her mouth. Once, the woolly mammoth with its white, curled tusks and elephant-like trunk drank the waters of the spring. But mammoths no longer walked the earth and bears, otters, mountain lions, herons, ducks, and muskrats were common now.

Refreshed by the cold, clear water, the coyote moved with certainty—and urgency. She found the den she had dug in the soft earth only the week before. The tunnel of the burrow opened into a small space, just large enough for the coyote to turn around. She curled up in the cool, dry darkness and waited.

The next day, a male coyote approached the spring. Like the female, he lowered his head and lapped at the clear water. Suddenly, the female coyote burst from the reeds that surrounded the spring. She raced at him. He stiffened. Her yellow eyes burning, she danced about him, licked his muzzle, and tapped his shoulder with her forepaw. He accepted his mate's attention with great dignity.

He walked away from her and investigated the burrow from which she had come. Sticking his head into the hole, he saw four squirming coyote pups, their eyes shut tight. These were his pups.

Turning around, he faced his mate. A strange feeling grew within his body. His stomach lurched and seemed to rise in his throat. Suddenly, he regurgitated the mice he had recently eaten. The female gratefully ate his offering. From the food her mate provided and the fresh spring water, the female would produce rich milk to feed the pups.

The male coyote mostly kept away from the family group. Although he would clean, care for, and play with the pups later, his main role now was as guard and hunter. After a few hours of rest, he was on the move again. He could eat almost anything: snails, beetles, frogs, skunks, birds and their eggs, grasshoppers, crickets, rats, berries, fish, and snakes. Depending on the prey, he could hunt either night or day.

The coyote mother had been wise in her choice of a burrow. She visited the spring to satisfy her great thirst to ensure that her milk flowed generously for her hungry pups.

In time, the pups opened their eyes. The burrow seemed to be shrinking, but it was really the pups that were growing larger and larger. The mother often took them on outings. One morning as they emerged from the burrow in single file behind their mother, she tensed. The pups felt the tension in her body as if it were their own. A low growl rose from her throat and the hair on her neck stood erect. She snapped at the pups. They immediately scampered back into the hole and huddled tightly together, still and quiet.

The female crept silently through the tall reeds surrounding the spring. Still concealed, she surveyed the pond. She could not understand what she saw, but the scent that came to her on the breeze made her shiver with fear. She had shared the spring waters with many creatures, but this one she did not know. It walked on two legs and moved in ways she did not recognize. It was abrupt and quick and

the sounds from its mouth were harsh and strange. As the coyote watched, the man built a fire and the orange and yellow flames were reflected in her fearful eyes.

Under the cover of darkness, the mother coyote moved her pups away from the spring and its new inhabitant. Her mate would find them in the other den she had dug weeks before: the escape den. Miles away, safe from the strange animal, she and her mate would raise this litter of pups and several more in the years that followed.

Over time, native people observed and learned from the ways of the coyote. They followed its trails to the sweet spring waters, and also dug wells in times of drought. It was the subject of many of their stories. And always they admired the coyote's ability to adapt to a world that changed too quickly.

The Cheyenne

The Cheyenne people once farmed, fished, and hunted in the area of the Great Lakes. Possibly because of conflicts with other groups, they moved to the Great Plains and hunted buffalo. They used every part of the buffalo for their survival—for food, clothing, shelter, and even for carrying water (the buffalo bladder).

The story that follows has been passed down among the Cheyenne Indians in more than one version. It tells of the Old Woman of the Spring, and of the return of the buffalo to the people.

The Cheyenne camped by water whenever possible. One day they set up their camp in a large circle where a spring gushed from the side of a hill. They had plenty of sweet water from the spring to drink and bathe in, but they were hungry. The buffalo had disappeared.

In the morning, many people gathered at the center of the camp to watch the men play a game of skill called ring and javelin. A young man from the south side of the camp joined the group. His body was painted yellow. He wore a yellow feather in his hair and held a buffalo robe around himself. As he watched the men trying to throw sticks through the rolling hoop, he caught sight of another young man dressed exactly like himself. This man had come from the north side of the camp.

The men moved toward each other through the crowd and finally came face to face. "You're dressed exactly like me," the man from the south said. "No, you are dressed like me," the man from the north said. Each shared the story of how he came to be dressed in this way.

As they spoke, a crowd gathered. The two men explained that each of them had separately entered the spring that flowed from the hillside and had been instructed to dress in this fashion. They agreed to enter the spring together this time.

The two men boldly entered the spring and discovered a large cave. An old woman sat by the entrance of the cave and she was cooking. In one pot was buffalo meat and in another corn. "Come sit by me," she invited them.

The two men sat. They said, "Our people are hungry; we have come to you to help us find food."

Stirring the pots, the old woman nodded her head. She offered them meat and corn from the two pots. They ate and ate, but when they were finished the pots were as full as if nothing had ever been taken from them.

Now the old woman said, "Look to the south." The two men did as she asked and saw a land rich with buffalo. "Look to the west," she directed. And when they did they saw mountains and valleys covered with all kinds of animals. Finally the old woman said, "Look to the north," and the two men saw fields of corn.

The old woman continued. "Tonight I will restore the buffalo to you." She gave them some seed corn and told them how to plant it. She also gave them meat and corn to feed their people and specific instructions on how the food should be eaten.

After paying close attention to the woman's words, the two men carried the food and seed corn through the spring. When they emerged on the other side, they were painted red. Even the feathers in their hair had changed to red.

The hungry people obeyed the words of the old woman and ate the food as directed. The two pots provided enough food for everyone in the camp.

Satisfied, the people returned to their own lodges, but each man, woman, and child closely watched the spring. Their attention was soon rewarded. Suddenly a buffalo leaped out of the spring. Shaking the water from its thick brown fur, it jumped and rolled in the grass and then returned to the spring. Soon another buffalo emerged, and then another and another. Pretty soon, the buffalo came so quickly that the people could no longer keep count.

All night the buffalo followed, one after another, from the waters of the spring. In the morning, the people looked around them and saw a land covered with buffalo. They rejoiced because their children would no longer cry from hunger. For years after that, the Cheyenne people hunted successfully and were fed, clothed, and sheltered by the buffalo of the Great Plains.

Soldier

As the population of the United States grew and as people spread throughout the country, sometimes there were conflicts, resulting from disagreements over land, lifestyles, and personal freedoms. The Civil War—the war fought between people from the northern and southern states of the United States—divided not only the country, but also many families.

This story shows how springs have provided refuge even during times of conflict. These special places remind us that regardless of our differences, we are all connected through water.

Winston studied the small, ragged piece of paper pinned to the blue uniform jacket of his best friend, Jack. Winston had long ago removed the strip of paper from his own chest. The fighting was over now. He believed that Jack continued to wear the scrap as a kind of talisman, a token to bring him good luck. Throughout the war, soldiers had often pinned these pieces of paper to their uniforms before going into battle; if a man died, he would be identified by the information scrawled on the scrap of paper.

Winston looked around at the lush green landscape. It was springtime and, in spite of the terrible things he had seen and experienced, his heart was light. He was going home.

He and his small command of soldiers had stopped at this wooded spring to fill their canteens with its sweet waters and to rest before they began their journey home. The soldiers were pleasantly surprised when women from the farmhouse on the property of the spring brought them warm loaves of homemade bread from the farm ovens.

Winston sat alone by the spring, marveling at the clear waters. As he tipped his head back and drank from the canteen, he thought he had never tasted anything better in his whole life. He hoped that he would hang on to this one thing the war had taught him—to be grateful for the small gifts that come our way: a refreshing drink of water, warm bread, the laughter of friends, a letter from home.

From his pocket, Winston took the tattered letter he had carried with him for the last several months. He skimmed its contents for the hundredth time, his attention always focused on one specific paragraph, the last:

My heart aches for the division this war has created in our own family. Like this great country, we too are split, one brother that fights for the North and one for the South. Your brother never had your courage; he chose based on what others believed. Perhaps it is particularly poignant because you and William are twins. I love both of you equally; for the heart of this family, like the heart of this country, must have forgiveness and love for all its members. When the war is over, come home. Let us in a new way build this family, and this country, together again.   Mother

As Winston folded the letter and replaced it in the inside pocket of his jacket, he thought of his twin and smiled. As boys, they had hunted together in the forests of Pennsylvania and fished its streams and rivers. Jack had often joined them and was referred to by the family as the third twin. One of the best things the two brothers did together was to make music; their mother had taught them both the piano and they had picked up the harmonica and other instruments on their own.

Jack interrupted Winston's thoughts. "We're making camp east of the spring, Captain. I think most everyone is turning in; they're anxious for an early start tomorrow. Do you think it's necessary to post a watch?"

Winston had proven himself a good leader during the war, never asking a man to do what he would not first do himself. Winston

Jack grinned. "Wake me up for the second." He gave Winston an informal salute and walked back to the camp.

As Jack walked away, Winston returned to the thoughts that tumbled over and over in his brain. Was it possible that the war was over? Perhaps in time he would come to believe it and to feel safe again.

Winston watched the stars come out in the night sky and studied their reflection in the clear waters of the spring. He felt in his pocket for his harmonica and began to play a soothing tune.

Lost in his thoughts and his music, he played on, and the hours slipped by. Suddenly, he heard the distant sound of another harmonica, like a familiar voice. Had he fallen asleep at his post and entered a dream? No, he was wide-awake, for the full moon had risen and was now reflected in the pool of the spring.

He remained very still, afraid to alter by even a note the song he played in unison with the other harmonica. He must not break the spell; for as he continued to play the music of the other instrument drew closer to him. Closer and closer the music came as Winston focused on the reflection of the moon in the spring's pool.

Soon the music came from behind his left shoulder. In the pool, Winston saw the reflection of a man's face, similar to his own, only thinner and sadder. The song reached its final note and the two musicians held it in beautiful harmony, until they could hold it no longer.

Winston sat very still in the night quiet and studied his twin's reflection. As he turned, he saw the tattered gray of his twin brother's uniform—the uniform of the defeated South. Before either of them could speak, Jack stepped from the trees.

Now, the three men faced each other. In a dry, cracked voice, William said, "I'll only trouble you for a drink of water from the spring. I lost my canteen days ago. I promise I'll be on my way."

Before Winston could respond, Jack said abruptly, "No, William, you won't be on your way."

Winston tried to say something, but he couldn't seem to move or speak. Through their connection as twins, Winston felt William's shame as if it were his own. Although Winston had also felt the sting of William's betrayal when he chose to fight for the South instead of the North, it was really Jack with whom William would need to make amends.

In one powerful movement, Jack knelt beside the spring and filled his canteen with water. He stood and looked steadily at William for a long time. Then, as if making up his mind, he extended the canteen to the man in the gray uniform and said, "It's going to be a long walk home, William. You better take mine."

William lowered his head and said in a parched whisper, "I can never go home again, Jack. You of all people know that."

Jack looked steadily at William, "This war can free you too, William, from your own fears and doubts. You and Winston and me can go home—together."

And as Jack threw his powerful black arm around William's thin shoulders in a clasp of friendship, Winston began to believe that the war might really be over.

Settlers

Today, the ruts of wagon wheels are only memories on the well-worn trails that settlers followed from spring to spring on their journeys west. Communities grew up around these waters and many towns adopted the names of the springs that sustained them. This is a true story of Doby Spring and a man who hoped to claim it, despite the odds against him.

When Christopher Columbus Doby was fourteen years old, he left his home in North Carolina and traveled to South Texas to become a cowboy. He got a job driving longhorn cattle from South Texas to Dodge City, Kansas. Doby was part of a very colorful but short era in United States history—the western cattle drives.

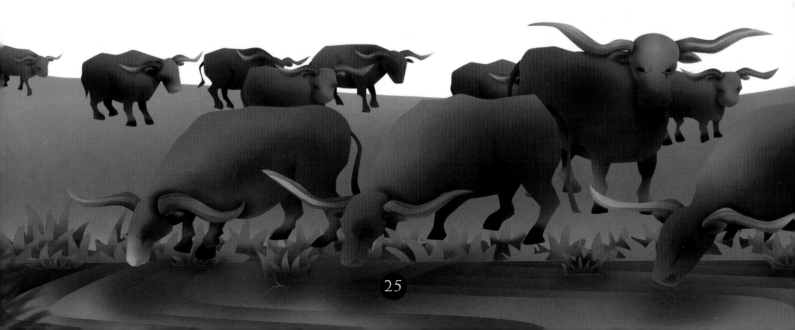

After the Civil War ended in 1865, some foods were in short supply throughout the country. Ranchers hired cowboys like Christopher Columbus Doby to be "drovers"—that is, to drive their longhorn cattle north from Texas across Oklahoma to the Kansas railroad towns. From there, the animals were shipped by train to northern and eastern markets.

Imagine Doby dressed in his cowboy garb. His Stetson hat with its wide brim kept sun and rain off his face, and the high dome cooled his head or held oats or water for his horse. He wore a bandanna knotted at the back of his neck, a sturdy cotton shirt, and wool vest; leather chaps protected his heavy pants from the brush and cactus, and high-heeled boots kept his foot in the stirrup.

Drovers like Doby pushed their longhorns on established cattle trails, generally from one source of fresh water to another. Now, there was one water hole that Doby particularly liked. It was originally called the Spring with the Big Tree. In fact, the first cowboy on the drive to see the cottonwood tree that towered above all of the other trees would cry out, "I see the big tree." Hearing this cry, the trail boss would remove his bandanna and drag it across the back of his sweaty neck in relief. It meant his cowboys and, more important, his thirsty cattle could drink their fill of the spring's clear waters.

By the early 1890s, Doby had worked his way up from drover to trail boss. Over the years, he had watched the railroad spread from Oklahoma into Texas. He had seen the fence lines grow as more farms and ranches were settled. He knew he was witnessing the final days of the great cattle drives.

So, Doby decided to participate in the Oklahoma Land Run of 1893. The government program had prospective settlers gather at established points. When the signal was given, they raced to stake their claim to land in north-central Oklahoma. Doby was one of about 50,000 settlers who took part in the run.

Doby had an advantage: he knew the value of the land of the Spring with the Big Tree and intended to lay claim to it. However, Doby also had competition: two big ranchers knew of the spring and they wanted it as well. Because they were men of means and believed that the fastest breed of horse would get them there first, each of them brought in a thoroughbred race horse.

The settlers gathered at the designated place. Amid the cacophony of men and women shouting, children crying, dogs barking, and horses squealing, Doby was mounted on a white cow pony named Eagle who stood steady. Eagle had been his partner for some time now. The horse had a stocky build: his chest was wide and deep and his hips were broad. His neck was thick, his head was a solid, blocky shape, and his ears were still, except to flick in Doby's direction when the cowboy spoke to his animal.

B. R. Grimes and Herring, the two well-to-do gentlemen, sat their thoroughbreds with pride. The sleek horses, their necks beautifully arched, their ears nervously twitching from front to back, pranced and sidestepped, lifting their long, slender legs gracefully. The two men may have looked in Doby's direction and scoffed at the mount he had selected, for they believed the horse dull, with neither the speed nor the stamina to live up to the grueling run.

Suddenly the signal was given and the horses and wagons were off in a blur of dust and tension. Eagle moved into an easy lope, while the thoroughbreds leaped into a powerful, fluid run that nearly snatched the breath from their riders. Casting dirt and rocks from their pounding hoofs, the thoroughbreds glided effortlessly past the steady Eagle. The men may have turned back to laugh at Doby and his blocky white horse, for they thought the man a fool who would race a cowpony against their elegant steeds.

With so little hope of winning, another man or woman might have quit, but Doby knew both men and horses and gently urged Eagle to hold the course. And the great lungs and, more important, the great heart of the little cowpony eagerly carried them forward.

Now a man who watched from a hill said that the thoroughbreds were a vision of beauty and power for the first three miles or so. They led the way as thousands of horses and riders fell far behind. But then the legs and lungs bred for the athletic sprint began to fail. Though Grimes and Herring used every means available to urge their mounts forward, their efforts were to no avail. As the stocky cowpony passed the thoroughbreds—white with foam—their chests heaving, did the little horse feel some satisfaction? Likely not, for cowponies are not a prideful breed and there was yet a long way to go.

Like his horse, Doby kept his focus on the course. They had three miles behind them and another twenty-five to go. But within hours, that scruffy white cowpony without a murmur of protest carried Doby over the rough and rocky terrain to the Spring with the Big Tree. There, the weary but grateful cowboy laid claim to the land.

Doby and his son built a dugout by hand. Soon the rest of Doby's family joined him. He and his wife raised ten children by the Spring with the Big Tree. Local people who remember say that Doby would have his children hold hands and make a circle around that great cottonwood tree. But the trunk of the tree was so large that the children, even as they grew, could not stretch to close the circle.

The Spring with the Big Tree was renamed Doby Spring. Located in the northwest corner of Oklahoma, it provides water for the nearby city of Buffalo. You can visit the spring, but you will not be able to find it by sighting the great cottonwood tree. In the early 1900s, the tree was split in half by lightning and died. However, people in Oklahoma are occasionally overheard saying, "I want to get back to Buffalo to get a good drink of Doby spring water."

President

Since early times, people throughout the world have believed that the waters of some springs can cure illness or, at the very least, make them feel better. In the United States, in the late 1800s, presidents, poets, movie stars, famous baseball players, and others "took the waters" and vacationed at elaborate resorts built at these springs.

The story that follows takes place in the early 1900s. It is fictional but the theme of the story is close to our hearts, the love of family—a love that for many of us includes the family dog.

"Daniel, if we aren't back in our beds before mother and father return from the ball, we'll be severely punished!" Liana spoke with all the authority of her fifteen years.

"Shh," her ten-year old brother said. "And don't call me Daniel. My name is Danny, unless I'm in trouble, and then it's Daniel, but not until then. Quick, close the door behind you."

The sound of the heavy door closing echoed loudly in the glass and marble room. Danny and Liana froze and looked at each other in fear. For the moment, clouds concealed the full moon, and the room was dark despite its large windows

The silence was broken by a low whine.

"Turk! It's safe, boy, come here," Danny whispered. The old dog's toenails clicked in a slow but steady rhythm on the marble floor as he walked heavily to the boy's side. The dog leaned against Danny and his large tail thumped the small boy's legs. Danny leaned over and put his arms around Turk's neck. With happiness, the dog licked the boy's face.

Danny laughed. "I told you I'd take care of things, Turk. People come from all over to drink this water and they say it makes them feel better. Why, if it works for people, I bet it can work even better for dogs."

Liana felt sad. Turk had always been a part of their family and now he was old. He walked stiffly and could only fetch a stick once or twice before he had to rest. But Danny, Turk's staunchest defender, told everyone that fetching sticks was way beneath Turk's dignity. Something special existed between Danny and Turk. Everyone knew it.

"I wish we had brought a candle. It's so dark in here," Liana said. "Where is the spring?"

"Today I watched the waiter with the white towel over his arm who served the water. We just have to get to the hand pump behind the glass." Danny started to grope his way in the dark toward the glass case at the front of the room.

Suddenly the moon came out from behind the clouds. Moonlight flooded the Spring House as if lighting a stage in preparation for magical happenings. Danny and Liana smiled at each other. Anticipation filled them, a feeling like waking up on Christmas morning or the first day of summer vacation.

"Moonlight brings back any number of fine memories for me," a deep voice intoned. "But I believe my favorite is watching my herd of cattle under the great Dakota sky." A man rose from a wicker chair just to the left of the steps leading down into the Spring House.

Danny and Liana let out a shriek and Turk, the years dropping away, barked and snarled in defense of the children in his care.

"My apologies for startling you," the man said. He bent down on one knee and offered his open hand to Turk, who stiffly sniffed it, the hair still raised on the back of his neck. Then, finding things in order, he relaxed and licked the man's fingers.

"His name is Turk," Danny said shyly.

The man gently patted the old dog's head. "Turk . . . . I once knew a hunting dog by that name, a bloodhound. A wonderful animal—he could climb trees, you know. I watched him tree a lynx thirty feet above the ground, remarkable dog."

Recovering his dignity, Danny said, "Oh, Turk can do that. Except he climbs much taller trees."

"Danny!" Liana said sharply.

"Well, I'm not surprised," said the man. "Your Turk is a fine-looking dog."

Turning to Liana, he said, "It's rather late for you to be out alone. But I sense you're on a great adventure."

"Well, sir," Liana said, "my mother and father have come here to take the waters, and Danny thought if the water was good for people, it might help Turk. Papa told Danny before we came that he has picked out a new puppy for us, as Turk is old. But Danny stomped his foot and got angry at Papa and said he would have nothing to do with a new dog." Liana paused. "Danny is small, but he can be stubborn, sir."

The man smiled ever so slightly.

"And then Papa was upset and said Danny would have to do as he was told. Turk could go on holiday, but that would be the end of it. He explained that he loved Turk too, but that this way would be kinder to everyone."

The man removed his gold wire-rimmed glasses and cleaned them with a cotton handkerchief. He carefully replaced them and studied the boy and the dog.

ideals. Do you understand?"

Danny looked at the gentleman. "No, sir, I'm sorry. I don't see how that will help me to keep my dog."

The man nodded and smiled with understanding. "You know, I have a perfect horror of words that are not backed up by deeds."

"Yes, sir," Danny agreed seriously.

"What I'm saying is that instead of upsetting your father with angry words, show him that you are willing to take responsibility for Turk. Demonstrate that you have the patience to walk slowly by Turk's side on cold mornings when his joints are stiff, or to prepare special food for him. Tell your father that you will take responsibility for the dog's special needs as he grows older. And that when the time comes, you will let him go with the dignity and respect he deserves. "

"I can do that, sir." Danny's spirits lifted. He patted Turk's head as the dog responded by wagging his heavy tail.

"It's the doer who counts in the world, children, not the man who only writes or talks about how things should be done."

Liana retorted in a rush. "And there you have it; I suppose you believe that only men should be the doers in the world." An angry red blush colored the girl's cheeks.

The gentleman looked startled. "Not at all. And I apologize for any misunderstanding my words may have caused. Since my youth, I have always believed that women should have equal rights with men."

"Equal rights, but not equal work," Liana responded hotly.

Danny looked at the man. "Liana is upset because she wants to be a scientist and Papa has said that it is work for men only."

"Nonsense," the man replied. "I believe that women should have the right to vote, to own property, to enter any profession, and to stand on an equal footing with any man in that profession."

Liana opened her mouth with a further protest.

"And," the man continued, "to receive equal pay for equal work."

Liana gets the best grades in her class," Danny said proudly, "and so do I."

"Then stick by your ideals and try to live up to them. You know people always imagine that others have an easier time of it than they do. I have never envied a person who led an easy life. But I have envied those who led difficult lives, and led them well."

The man paused and looked at the expectant children. "Well, here we are talking the night away and not taking action ourselves. You believe the spring waters may help your dog." The man was thoughtful. "It's true, people travel to springs all over this country. They do believe the waters can cure them. Folks who have tried almost every spring and haven't found a cure are said to be 'down to their last resort.' But I imagine this is your first resort." The man smiled. "Did you know the Indians were the first people to use springs?"

"How do you know that?" asked Danny.

"Arrowheads and stone tools have been found at many springs."

The children's eyes grew wide.

"Well, enough talk. It's time for a little action. What do you say, Danny?"

"Yes, sir," the small boy responded solemnly.

"You two wait here with Turk. Put his bowl on the floor there. I'll just borrow that silver pitcher to fetch the water."

The two children watched the man enter the glass-enclosed area that housed the spring. Standing beside the small hand pump where the spring itself could be viewed through a clear glass cover, he pumped the silver handle carefully up and down. Soon the cold, clear water flowed into the pitcher directly from the spring below.

As the man approached the waiting children with the pitcher, Turk started to whine loudly. He shook slightly, as if he were cold.

"Turk, you're going to be fine," Danny soothed him.

Suddenly the door to the Spring House was thrown open. The light from a lantern flooded the room with its brightness.

Turk jumped to his feet with the fur raised on his back and neck and growled menacingly. He stood his ground between the children and the startled crowd at the door.

"Liana, Danny, we've found you!" a voice cried out.

"Mother? Papa?" Liana asked.

Turk wagged his tail as Liana and Danny's mother and father rushed to embrace them.

"You weren't in your beds when we went to check on you after the ball. Everyone at the resort has turned out to search for you. I am so thankful you are safe," their mother cried softly.

Danny and Liana's father cleared his throat. "You children have caused your mother considerable worry," he said sternly.

Suddenly the gentleman holding the silver pitcher interrupted. "I understand your concern; I have several dearly loved children of my own. But from my admittedly limited experience with your children, I believe they were well protected by the dog to whom you wisely entrusted them—Turk. And from what I have heard and seen tonight, this animal deserves a special place in

your home. He has earned it. And Danny has committed to care for Turk as he weakens with age. Indeed, you have a fine son who I believe will one day be a fine man." Proudly, Danny patted the old dog, who responded with a generous and loving tail wag.

The excited crowd had fallen silent at the man's words. In the years to come, Danny and Liana would tell their children and grandchildren about the look of astonishment on their parents' faces.

Finally the children's father said, "Mr. President, I . . . I couldn't agree more. Turk is indeed a special dog. Perhaps in fearing the sadness his loss would cause, I have been too hasty in my decision to replace him. Of course you are right, sir. Turk deserves our love. He will always have a special place in our home, as he does in our hearts." Looking perplexed, he paused. "But sir," he continued, "I am confused about the extraordinary events of this evening. You, the children, Turk, the Spring House . . . ?"

The pitcher of spring water in one hand, the President of the United States held up his other hand and smiled easily. "It's a long story, my good man. What do you say we share some of this water? I'd like to talk to you about Liana. I understand she wants to grow up to be a scientist. Now surely you support woman suffrage . . . ."

As Danny and Liana watched the crowd part for the President and their father to pass, they felt that everything was going to turn out just fine.

Theodore Roosevelt was the twenty-sixth president of the United States. One of the most popular presidents in American history, he was an avid outdoorsman and is reported to have occasionally "taken the waters" himself. He was the first president to focus the country on the need to conserve our precious natural resources like land, and water. His message is as meaningful today as it was in the early 1900s.

Roosevelt's greatness is timeless. He was a man of courage, determination, and integrity. Among his many accomplishments, he was a gifted father with a great love for his family. He took time even out of the presidency to read to and play with his children.

When he was traveling, Theodore Roosevelt wrote many wonderful letters to his children. He often illustrated them with line drawings. After reading from his autobiography, biographies, letters, and other material, I believe that if Theodore Roosevelt were to write a letter to children of the twentieth-first century, it might go something like this:

Dear Children:

When I was a small boy, I lived in New York City. And it was there in that great city that I first became interested in the natural world. One day, as I made my way up Broadway, I was thinking all kinds of boyish thoughts when my attention was suddenly drawn to something laid out on the curb. It was a shiny black seal, dead of course, but nonetheless fascinating. So out of place on that city street, the seal filled me with a sense of wonder and adventure. Where did it come from? What did it eat? The seal ignited within me an interest in the natural world that could never be extinguished.

I lived many roles in my life, including rancher, writer, soldier, governor, vice president, president, husband, and father. I loved my children. We read many great books together and had many grand adventures. On one occasion, when one of the children was ill, Algonquin the pony was taken in the White House elevator to the sick room for a visit. I know that Woodrow Wilson once called me a "great big boy." Well, perhaps I was, but I believe it was that attitude that allowed me to see life for what it was—a grand adventure.

When I was president, I used my power to focus the country on the need for stewardship for our natural resources. I told Congress that the forest and water problems were perhaps the most vital internal problems of the United States. During my term I helped to expand the national forests and to establish national parks, game refuges and other areas for the protection and conservation of our natural resources.

Well, my stories have been told. The time has come for you, the children of the twenty-first century, to live and tell your own. Learn from our mistakes and be good stewards of our natural resources, not only for yourselves, but also for the children who are not yet born.

I leave you with these final words I once said to the schoolchildren of Oyster Bay, New York. It was around Christmas time.

"There are two things that I want you to make up your minds to do; first, that you are going to have a good time as long as you live—I have no use for the sour-faced man—and next, that you are going to do something worthwhile, that you are going to work hard and do the things you set out to do."

Theodore Roosevelt
Twenty-sixth president of the United States
1901-1909

Spring Waters:
Myth and Legend

How often have you tossed a coin into a fountain and made a wish? This custom began thousands of years ago. Throughout time, people made offerings at springs and wells: they left gifts and hoped that they would receive good luck in return.

Although they came up with many interesting theories, earlier people did not understand how springs gushed from the earth. Why were some springs hot and some cold? How did springs bubble up in the middle of the desert? People did not believe that the water for springs came from rain and other forms of precipitation. In the 1600s, they thought that the water for springs came from holes in the ocean floor.

In the 1700s, Antonio Vallisnieri, a university president from Italy, observed the springs of the Alps and concluded that spring waters began with rainfall or snowmelt that seeped into the ground. His theory displaced the idea of holes in the ocean floor until 1977, when oceanographers discovered hot springs gushing from the floor of the sea!

Early people saw springs as a gift from Earth. Not only did they recognize that these waters satisfied their thirst; they also believed that certain spring waters cured disease and even healed the blind and the lame. Based on the life-giving waters that mysteriously flowed from under the ground, early people often attributed magical qualities to springs and told wonderful stories about them.

Pegasus

Greek mythology tells of a white, winged horse named Pegasus. This beautiful wild horse lived by an enchanted pool on a mountain called Helicon.

The horse had made the U-shaped pool himself, with one stamp of his hoof. It was fed by cool spring waters that bubbled up into it. A young prince named Bellerophon tamed the horse with a golden bridle that he received from a goddess. With the help of Pegasus, the prince killed a horrible monster called Chimera and won the hand of the only daughter of King Iobates of Lycia, an ancient country to the north of Greece.

Odin, the Supreme Norse God

Some spring waters were believed to offer wisdom to those who sampled them. The Norse god Odin was desperate for knowledge. He appealed to Mimir the Wise who controlled the sacred water. Mimir agreed to share the water with Odin if the god put out one of his own eyes. Odin thought about Mimir's request. If he could not understand what he was seeing, what was the good of his sight anyway? He put out his eye, drank from the spring, and received the wisdom that helped him to defeat giants that were threatening heaven and earth.

Fountain of Youth

It was often told that somewhere on Earth was a spring whose waters made the old young and the weak strong. Some legends maintained that when old men or women looked upon the surface of this spring, they saw the faces of their youth reflected back to them. Although explorers searched the world for such a spring, it was never found. Imagine how people must have longed for spring waters that would restore their youth or health in a time when old age came at forty and there were few medicines for pain or cures for diseases.

Native Americans and Springs

Artifacts left by early Indians have been found at springs throughout North America. Native Americans considered many springs special and left offerings of tiny pottery vessels, stone beads, and the bones of animals. Some researchers believe that the Indians left pottery to remind the rulers of the waters of the world to pour the precious water from their vessels upon the lands of the people.

The Spanish word *ojo* (meaning eye) is in the names of many springs in the southwest. This may come from the Zuni belief that the gods peered through springs to see the upper world.

The Hopi Indians have a beautiful and natural connection with their springs. The rich plant and animal life—dragonflies, cranes, butterflies, and reeds—that surrounds the pools of springs speaks to the Hopi of the life-giving force of water. Springs, water, and rain are common themes in stories, personal names, ritual costumes, and songs. Special ceremonies are often performed at springs. The Flute Dance is devoted specifically to springs and their well-being. At certain times, the Hopi leave feathered prayer sticks embedded in the banks of springs. Sometimes the Hopi carry water, clay, tree branches, or reeds from springs back to their villages to use in special ceremonies.

Even in water-rich areas such as the Pacific Northwest, some Native American creation myths recall the beginning of springs. According to one of these legends, in the past, all water was salt water. However, Raven discovered a powerful being who had a well of fresh water. Savoring the taste of this sweet water, Raven stole a beakful and flew for home. As he escaped, drops of fresh water dripped from his beak. Wherever the drops fell, lakes, rivers, and springs appeared on the land.

Many of the springs used by early Indians still provide drinking water for people today. In California, Calistoga bottled water is taken from a geyser originally discovered by the Wappo Indians.

Great Bear Spring in New York State is associated with the Onondaga Indians with whom the legend of Hiawatha originated. According to tradition, the father of Hiawatha was hunting when he met and overcame a huge bear . . .

Thus was slain the Mishe-Mo-Kwa,
He is the Great Bear of the Mountains

After his struggle with the bear, the hunter sought the spring and drank. Giving thanks, he named it the Mishemokwa (Great Bear) Spring in honor of his victory.

It is believed that Native Americans were the first to drink and bathe in the hot springs at Lake Arrowhead, California. The Indians sighted a natural rock formation high in the San Bernardino Mountains that directed them to the source. The rock was in the shape of an arrowhead that pointed to the bottom of a hill where many unusual springs flowed. The arrowhead is still visible today.

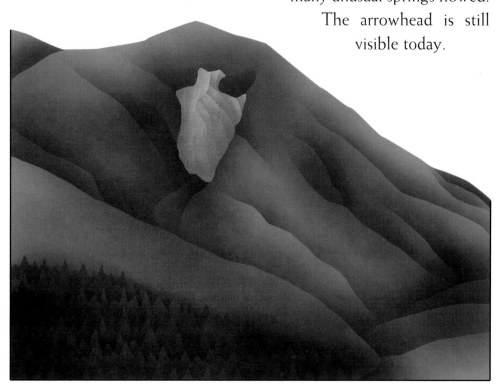

An Incredible Journey

As a liquid, gas, or solid, powered by the sun and the force of gravity, water travels over, under, and above the surface of Earth through the water cycle. Spring waters are part of this incredible journey. With your family and friends, become water molecules and evaporate into the clouds, remain frozen in a glacier, or flow from a mountain spring. Ready, set, evaporate! Condense! Melt! Freeze!

Players: One to four, shrunk to the size of water molecules.
Goal: The first player to visit and write down all ten places and return to the clouds wins! If playing alone, set a timer and visit as many places as you can in three minutes.
You Need: Scissors, pieces of paper, notepad, pencil, paper sack, playing pieces (pebbles, buttons, or seeds), "An Incredible Journey" playing board.
Before Playing: Cut paper into six squares, number them from 1 to 6, and place in a sack.

Here's How to Play:
• Place playing pieces on the Spring to start.
• Have first player draw a number from the sack. Read directions by the Spring and move your marker to the location indicated. Example: if you draw "2," move to Lake.
• On a notepad, write or draw Lake.
• Return the number to the bag and give it to the next player.
• When your notepad shows that you have visited all ten places, keep playing until you return to the Clouds.

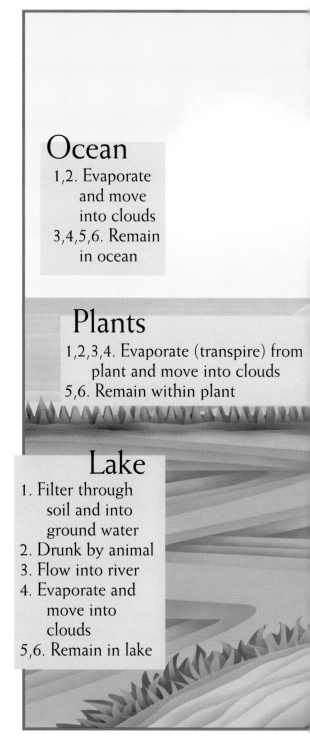

Ocean
1,2. Evaporate and move into clouds
3,4,5,6. Remain in ocean

Plants
1,2,3,4. Evaporate (transpire) from plant and move into clouds
5,6. Remain within plant

Lake
1. Filter through soil and into ground water
2. Drunk by animal
3. Flow into river
4. Evaporate and move into clouds
5,6. Remain in lake

Clouds

1. Condense and fall on soil
2. Condense and fall as snow on glacier
3. Condense and fall into lake
4,5. Condense and fall into ocean
6. Remain as part of water drop, stay in clouds

Glacier

1. Melt and filter into ground water
2. Evaporate and move into clouds
3. Melt and flow into river
4,5,6. Remain frozen in glacier

Spring

1. Flow into river
2. Flow into lake
3. Evaporate and move into clouds
4. Filter through soil and into ground water
5. Absorbed by roots of plant
6. Remain in spring pool

Animal

1,2. As waste products, move into soil
3,4,5. Evaporate and move into clouds
6. Stay within animal

Ground Water

1. Filter into river
2. Naturally flow to surface as spring
3. Filter into lake
4,5,6. Remain in ground water

River

1. Flow into lake
2. Filter through soil and into ground water
3. Flow into ocean
4. Drunk by animal
5. Evaporate and move into clouds
6. Remain in river

Soil

1. Absorbed by roots of plants
2. Drain into river
3. Filter through soil into ground water
4,5. Evaporate and move into clouds
6. Remain in puddle on soil surface.

Spring Secrets

Early people often associated springs with spirits and gods. Because the water moved, the ancients believed that it had a spirit. And, because of the powers of the spirit, the spring was thought to be magical.

Even today, you may be walking in the woods with your friends and come across a spring. Like people from long ago, you might turn to your friends and say, "It's magic!" Or, like modern-day scientists called hydrogeologists, you could investigate further.

Your mission will be to explain how a spring works. Just as people in earlier times did, you may wonder how a spring can flow from the ground when the area in which it is found is dry, even desert-like. How can a spring continue to flow when it has not rained in the area for a long time?

To help you uncover the secrets of springs, you will be provided with questions. The pictures, diagrams, and suggested hands-on investigations that follow will help you answer the questions. In building your understanding of springs, you will work from things you know and can see (like water moving on the surface of the land) to understand what you cannot see (water under the ground). Let's begin.

Wondrous Springs

Where does the water that feeds a spring come from?

Look at the picture titled *Wondrous Springs* (previous page). This picture shows a spring on the surface of the land. But where does the water come from that feeds the spring?

From this picture you may conclude that water flowing

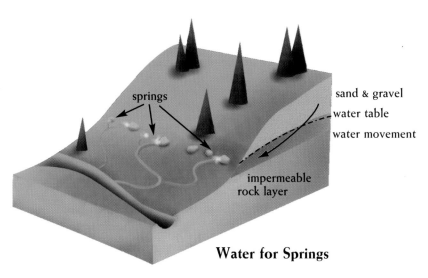

Water for Springs

from springs is water that runs off the land after a rain or perhaps comes directly from under the ground. Like the early people who discovered springs, you do not have enough information to answer the question.

Now look at the diagram labeled *Water for Springs*. Notice the springs located at the bottom of the hill. This diagram is a picture of water under the ground and how it may connect with water on the surface of the land. Just from looking at this picture, can you imagine where water for springs comes from? (Hint: The dashed line labeled "water table" indicates that the soil and rock below the line are saturated with water.) Write down what you think, fold the paper in half, and put it away for now. Then read on!

Underground Water

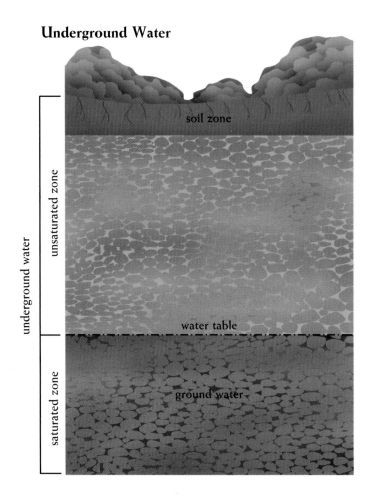

soil zone

underground water

unsaturated zone

water table

saturated zone

ground water

What is water under the ground called?

Imagine digging a hole in the ground. As you dig deeper you may find that the soil changes color. The soil may have been deposited thousands of years ago by running water, a retreating glacier, or even the wind. Eventually you reach gravel.

Finally, after digging for a long time, you may reach bedrock, a fairly solid mass of rock that makes up the crust of the earth. (In some places you would not have to dig at all because the bedrock is at the surface.) So, as you dig down into the ground you may see different layers of soil, sand, gravel, and rock.

Imagine when you first started digging, the soil was moist; it had rained only yesterday and the earth still held soil moisture or soil water. However, as you dug deeper, the hole eventually filled with water: ground water. *Ground water is the water found under the ground in the spaces between soil particles or in the pores, cracks, and fractures in rock material in the saturated zone.*

Look at the diagram titled *Underground Water.* You can see from this picture that not all underground water is ground water. Water in the unsaturated zone is not ground water. Why? (Because the spaces between soil particles are still partly filled with air, not water.) Ground water is found where all the spaces in the sand, gravel, or rock material are saturated (filled) with water. In general, water in the saturated zone is the only underground water that supplies wells and springs.

Do you believe that water can move into the spaces between soil particles?

Fill a plastic cup or glass one-half full with sand or soil. Pour a cup of water on top of the soil. Watch what happens. If you are not actually conducting this investigation, think about what might happen. If water can move by passing through the spaces between soil particles, then the water should move downward through the sand. If there were no spaces between sand particles, then the liquid would have no place to go and would pool on top of the sand. What happens?

The water moves down through the soil in the cup, until all the air in the spaces between the soil particles has been replaced with water. When all of the spaces have been filled, the soil is saturated with water. Continue to fill the cup of soil with water. How will you know when the soil is saturated? Water will pool on top of the soil layer because it has no place else to go.

The drawing labeled *Ground Water on the Move* shows soil particles with interconnected spaces that scientists call pore spaces. Water molecules, pushed along by gravity, and/or other forces wind their way through this maze.

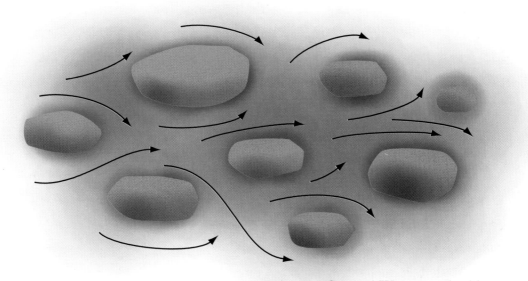

Ground Water on the Move

Can water move through all materials at the same rate?

As the soil and rock on the earth's surface vary, so does the material underground. There are different types of soil and rock, and they occur in different thicknesses. These different materials and thicknesses have a lot to do with how ground water moves.

Sometimes these materials are permeable; they allow water to pass through them. Think of how the water moved through the sandy soil in the cup experiment. The soil is a permeable material. But what if you poured water on a solid rock, like granite? Would the water soak into the rock? Probably very little of it because, except for a few small fractures or cracks, the rock is impermeable.

Water will also move at different rates through different materials. Place sand, gravel, and clay in separate clear containers with holes punched in the bottom. Pour equal amounts of water in each cup and observe the rate at which water moves through the different materials. You will probably find that it moves the fastest through gravel and slowest through clay.

Where is ground water located or stored under the ground?

Ground water is often contained in an aquifer. An aquifer is an underground layer of saturated sand, gravel, or other rock material

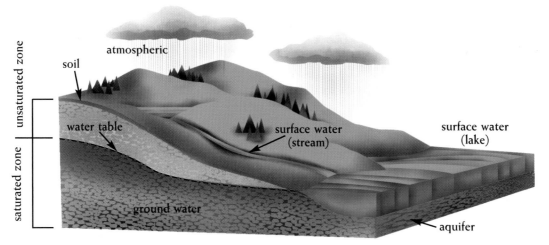

Atmospheric, Surface, Soil, and Ground Water

56

that yields significant quantities of water that may be pumped to the surface for use by people, livestock, or watering crops. You, your family, and your community may depend on an aquifer for your water supply. Although some towns and cities rely on surface water from streams and ponds, other communities depend on ground water, and some cities tap both.

How does ground water move?

Let's use something you know to learn about something you may not know. Think about how water moves on the surface of the land. We can see how water flows in rivers, creeks, and streams.

Place a cookie sheet flat on the kitchen counter. Sprinkle water on the sheet. What does it do? More than likely the water beads up or pools. Now lift one end of the cookie sheet. What happens? At some point the water will flow down the sheet in a small stream.

On the surface of the land, water flows downhill in rivers, streams, or tiny rivulets. Why? On earth, gravity pulls on you and everything else. Gravity pulls on water and causes it to flow downhill on the surface of the earth. Of course water may also soak into the soil and not flow along the surface at all, especially on level ground.

But how does water flow underground? The answer to this question is complex. It depends on the type of material the water is moving through, pressure, and other factors, including gravity—even ground water is strongly influenced by gravity. In fact, gravity is the main driving force in ground water movement. Since there are no "hills" under the ground, we say that ground water moves down-gradient rather than downhill. This means that water in the pore spaces of sand, gravel, clay or other materials and the cracks in rocks moves downward until it meets an impermeable layer. Then, the ground water may flow in another direction, following the path of least resistance.

Examples of Different Springs

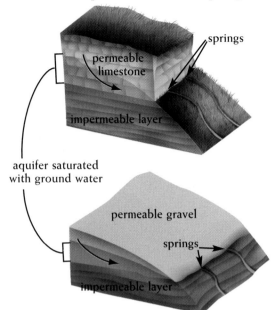

permeable limestone

springs

impermeable layer

aquifer saturated with ground water

permeable gravel

springs

impermeable layer

How does water become ground water?

We know that ground water is found under the ground and that it moves through soil, sand, or rock material in the spaces between particles or in the cracks and fissures in rocks. But how does water become ground water? Look at the drawing labeled *Atmospheric, Surface, Soil, and Ground Water.* (p.56) Can you identify four places where water exists in this drawing?

Water is found in the atmosphere, on the surface of the land (i.e., lakes and streams), in the soil layer (soil moisture), and, finally, in ground water.

Water exists in the atmosphere as vapor, rain, snow, or as other forms of precipitation. It falls on the surface of the land, perhaps in a lake, river, or ocean, and becomes part of that body of water. Sometimes it falls on the rock of a mountaintop and drains off into a stream, lake, or the soil below.

Sometimes it falls directly on soil. As we saw in the cup of soil investigation, the water moves downward through the soil. However, it may not become ground water. It may be held in the soil until it finally evaporates, or it may be taken up by plant roots and eventually returned to the atmosphere. On the other hand, gravity may continue to move the water downward through soil and rock material to a level where all spaces, cracks, and fractures are saturated. Now it has become ground water.

**How does ground water move to
the surface of the land to form a spring?**

Look at the two diagrams that illustrate how springs are formed. In addition to springs, what features do they have in common?

In both examples ground water is moving down-gradient through permeable materials until it comes to the surface of the land where a spring is formed. In each case, an impermeable layer (a layer that allows little or no water to move through it) keeps the ground water from moving further down-gradient.

Look again at the two diagrams. Ground water is always seeking the easiest way to flow down-gradient and, in this case, the easiest route is to flow out of the aquifer and onto the surface of the land.

Think about the questions and answers you have worked through. Take out the piece of paper on which you wrote your answer to the question, "Where does the water come from that feeds a spring?" You may want to change or refine your answer.

Compare your final answer to the definition of a spring: A spring occurs where ground water naturally meets the surface of the land. Was your answer more complete after you had conducted the investigations and reviewed the pictures?

A special kind of spring called an artesian spring brings ground water that is under pressure to the surface.

**Like early people, you might ask,
"How can a spring flow where it is dry, like in the
desert, or where it has not rained recently?"**

Consider the different diagrams you have seen of springs. Where does water enter the system? Water enters the system in a recharge area that may be miles from the spring itself. Waters that feed springs may actually travel several miles under the ground from the recharge area, which may be in an environment that has received rainfall.

Are springs always the same temperature?

What do you notice about the names of these springs found throughout the United States: Circle Hot Spring, Alaska; Hot Springs, South Dakota; Mammoth Hot Springs, Yellowstone National Park, Wyoming? Each name includes a description of the temperature of the spring—hot! In Yellowstone National Park, and other parts of the world, molten rock is closer to the earth's surface and heats the rock that warms the ground water which bubbles from a spring. On the other hand, areas with different geology have springs that are icy cold!

Why are ground water and springs important to you?

If you live in a rural area, it is likely that your family has a well. Now a well, like a spring, taps ground water. What makes a well different from a spring? The definition of a spring, says that ground water *naturally* meets the surface of the land.

How does ground water get to the surface in a well? Look at the picture titled *More Than a Wishing Well*. An electric pump moves ground water up from a well. In some areas, windmills, powered by the

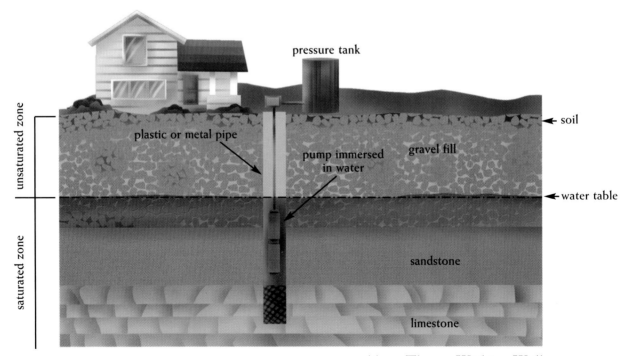

More Than a Wishing Well

wind, provide the energy to pump ground water. Your grandparents may have used a hand pump or perhaps brought water up from the well with a crank and bucket. Methods for getting water from a well vary around the world.

Hand Pump

People in rural areas aren't the only ones who use ground water; people living in cities or urban areas do too. Many cities rely on huge well fields (many individual wells in one area) to provide for their water needs. Often they use both surface water and ground water resources.

Electric Pump

In some special places, spring water is bottled and sold for drinking. Generally these springs are found in natural areas that have not been extensively developed. Hydrogeologists are hired to look for springs in areas where there is not a heavy concentration of people or human activity. Although other factors must be considered, these pristine areas often produce excellent water.

Windmill

However, a spring that provides drinking water must be more than just free of contaminants. When chemists analyze the water, it must be balanced in minerals: it cannot have too much sodium or too little magnesium or calcium. Like the story of *The Three Bears*, there cannot be too little or too much, the water chemistry must be "just right", and the source must provide that balance consistently.

Understanding the science of springs does not detract from their beauty or sense of magic. Tracing a stream back to its source and finding that it begins as a small spring bubbling from the ground is an experience that will stay with you forever. And springs are everywhere! Like early Native Americans, explorers, or settlers perhaps you and your parents or friends can discover a spring of your very own.

Crank & Bucket Well

Healthy Water, Healthy

The Blue Planet

Earth is often called the blue planet. Color photographs of Earth taken from space show mainly shades of blue. This is not surprising, since water circulating in oceans or frozen in ice fields covers about 71 percent of the earth. However, not all the water on the planet is available for use by plants, people, or other animals.

Imagine that 100 drops represent all the water in the world. How many drops do you think would be taken up by the salt water found in the oceans, the seas, and some lakes and rivers? The answer is 97 drops. Three drops represent Earth's fresh water. However, much of the fresh water is frozen in ice caps and glaciers: 2 ½ drops are frozen. This leaves about ½ drop of fresh water. But not all of this water is available; much of it is deep underground or trapped in soil. The very tip of one water drop represents potable (drinkable) fresh water.

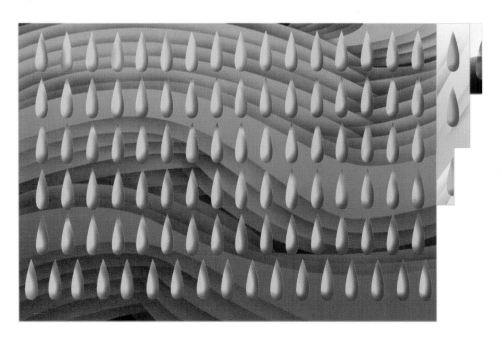

Although this does not seem like much water, on a global scale there is plenty of water for everyone on the planet. In fact, this amount of water exceeds what all 6 billion people on earth require in their lifetime. So, why does more than one-third of the world's population not have access to clean water?

Climate varies depending where you live. Some people live in hot, dry areas like Yuma, Arizona, which receives about 3 inches of rain a year. Others live in places like New Orleans, Louisiana which receives over 60 inches per year. Water is not distributed evenly over the planet. The availability of water also depends on other factors such as how water is used, the technology available to treat water, and the water conservation practices of a community.

Conserve Water!

Although domestic water use takes up only a very small percentage of all water used, it is still important to conserve water in our homes. Today every American uses 50 to 100 gallons of water daily. Our grandparents used much less water. Wasting water is also wasting money. We pay for water to be managed, transported, and treated. Communities that conserve water have often been able to keep taxes down by not having to build new and improved treatment plants or other facilities.

Water for all water users!

You may be surprised to learn all the ways that water is used. Look at the list below. Is there one item that does not require water for its production?

- blue jeans
- loaf of bread
- an automobile
- paper
- a cheeseburger

No! Each item in this list was produced with water. Look at the diagram *Water for all Water Users*. This shows the many water uses and how much water each requires. This picture is based on freshwater use in the United States and would look different if adapted to represent other parts of the world.

Try making a list of all the water uses you can think of in the categories shown in the diagram.

- Domestic (water for all the things you do at home, i.e., drinking, bathing, cooking)
- Commercial (water for restaurants, motels, offices)
- Industry (water to produce metals, wood, paper goods, gasoline)
- Thermoelectric (water for producing electrical power from burning coal and other fuels)
- Mining (water for extracting materials from the earth and washing the ore)
- Irrigation (water for growing crops)
- Livestock (water for cows, chickens, and horses and for processing meats, poultry, eggs, and milk)

Other water uses that are not pictured include recreation, fish and wildlife, navigation, and hydroelectric. These uses are very important, too, but in general they are considered nonconsumptive—they do not remove water from the source.

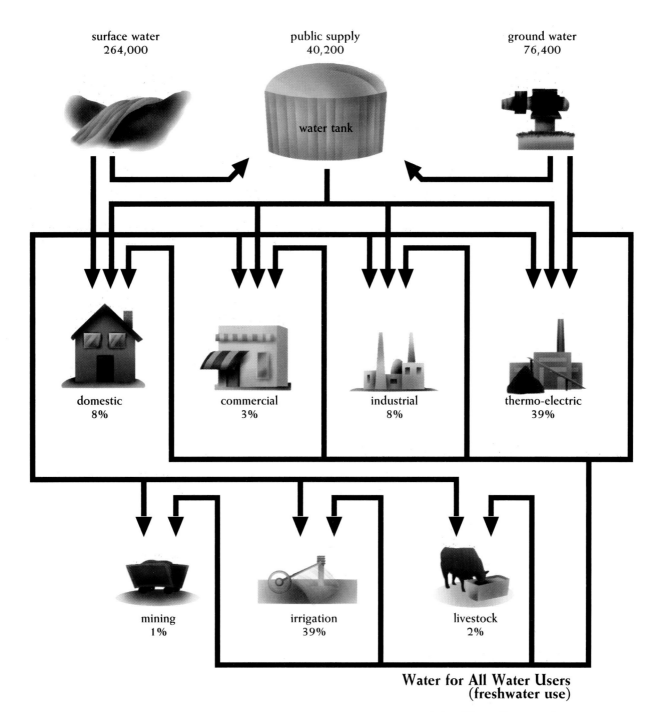

surface water
264,000

public supply
40,200

ground water
76,400

water tank

domestic
8%

commercial
3%

industrial
8%

thermo-electric
39%

mining
1%

irrigation
39%

livestock
2%

Water for All Water Users
(freshwater use)

unit is million gallons per day.
The numbers are rounded and about 6,000 million gallons per day
are not available from Public supply because of system losses.

Source: wwwga.usgs.gov/edu/graphicshtml/summary95.html

65

Water users in the United States withdraw about 340,400 million gallons per day of freshwater. Sources of freshwater include surface water (about 264,000 million gallons per day) and ground water (76,400 million gallons per day). Some surface water and ground water are treated and become part of the public supply (about 40,200 million gallons per day).

Look at the domestic water use in the diagram. Notice the pipe leading from surface water. Few people take their water directly from surface sources such as rivers and streams and use it without treatment. The pipe from ground water shows that water for domestic use can come directly from ground water, for example from a well. The third pipe shows the water that comes into homes from the public supply; most homes in the United States have their water delivered through pipes from the local water treatment facility.

Water users vary greatly in the amount of water they require. For example, domestic water use represents only about 8 percent of the 340,400 million gallons per day of freshwater; a small amount of this is actually drinking water. Irrigation, which is critical for producing the food we eat, and thermoelectric, that produces electrical power, each use 39 percent of available water. As you carefully study the chart, you will see that different water uses not only require different amounts of water but also vary in their use of public supply and ground water and surface water sources.

Healthy Water

When we think about water use, we sometimes think only about water quantity—that is, having enough water for our needs. But water quality is extremely important! The water we drink must be free of disease-causing agents, and chemicals must be at acceptable levels. In fact, throughout the world about 80 percent of all diseases, such as cholera and hepatitis A, are water-related. Many of these illnesses are spread by water contaminated with sewage.

Government agencies monitor surface and ground water supplies, set the standards for safe drinking water, and recommend practices to improve water quality. Did anyone ever say, "You're one in a million"? Scientists measure and report water contaminants in parts per million, parts per billion, and parts per trillion. Although these may seem like extremely small concentrations, the toxicity of some chemicals can cause health problems at very low levels.

Spring water that is bottled for drinking is also carefully monitored. Before selecting a spring for bottled water, geologists study the area and the water to ensure that the flow is consistently clean and healthy. Even after the site is selected and water is being bottled, chemists continue to test the water several times every day to ensure its purity. A large number of people manage, monitor, and protect the source to assure the highest possible water quality.

Some people drink bottled water for its clean, nonchemical taste, while others drink it for what it contains, such as minerals. Depending on the type of rock material the water moves through, it may pick up minerals on its way back to the surface. For example, water that passes through limestone may pick up calcium. Also, areas of lava rock produce carbonated springs. Sometimes carbonation is added to the water by bottlers. (Carbonation is what gives water its fizz.)

As water moves through the water cycle, it can be cleaned naturally. Sand, gravel, rock, and other materials may remove contaminants as the water percolates through them.

Other natural processes break down contaminants as well. However, in areas where large numbers of people are concentrated, it is necessary to give nature a helping hand. Water is first cleaned at water treatment plants to make it safe. After being used, it is called wastewater and is treated at wastewater treatment plants before it is released back into rivers, lakes, oceans, or other bodies of water.

Healthy People

We know that it is important to drink good quality water, but how much of it should we drink each day and why? Although most of us can get a drink of water fairly easily, many people go through their day dehydrated. Our bodies need water to function properly. Sometimes when we feel tired, it is because we have not gotten enough sleep, but fatigue can also result if we are not properly hydrated.

The human body is about 65 to 70 percent water and the human brain is about 75 percent water! Did your brain get enough to drink today? Although humans are able to live for about one month without food, they can only live three to four days without water. Doctors tell us that we should drink at least eight glasses of water daily. If you are exercising hard or if you are sick, you may need to drink even more water.

Study the basketball player and learn the many ways water works for you.

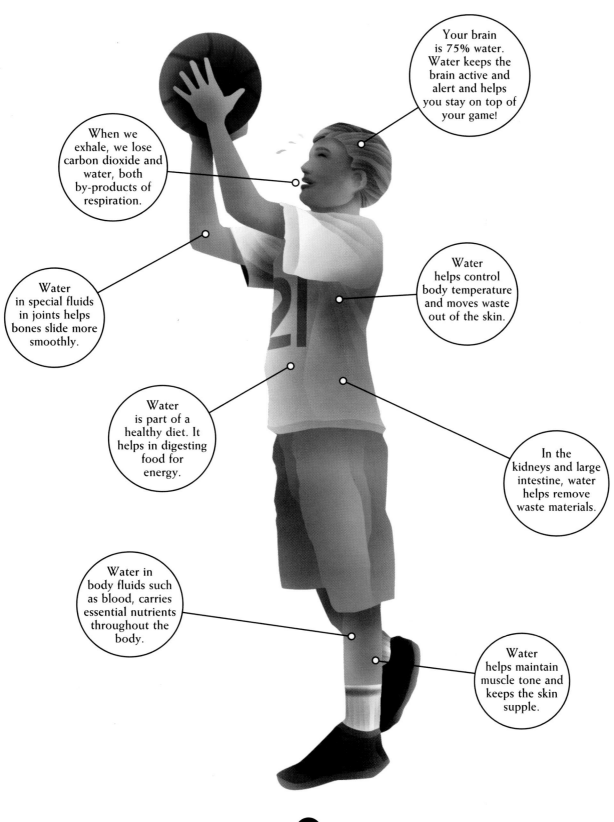

Notes
Gathering Places

Coyote

This story is based on the natural history of the coyote. The use of springs by wildlife was documented in the book *Springs of Texas* by Gunnar Brune. In the chapter "Prehistoric Setting of Springs" Brune maintains that before humans arrived in the New World, plants and animals gathered at and thrived around springs.

Native Americans: The Cheyenne

There is evidence that Native Americans used springs all over the country. Grinding holes where native people ground acorns and other nuts, grains, and beans have been found by some springs. There are boulders with smooth tops where they rubbed animal skins to remove the hair and fat. Grooves were cut in the rocks for straightening arrows. Often the Indians left arrowheads or stone tools behind.

Soldier

The inspiration for this story came from the Hoffman Spring Manual, an in-house publication:

"Legend has it that weary soldiers would seek refuge on their long journeys at the Mosser Estate. They would camp on the property and were fed by the women of the family who baked bread for them in the farm bake oven and they were refreshed with glasses of fresh mountain spring water from the spring (Hoffman's Spring) located on the property. The soldiers were then sent on their way with renewed energy and full canteens to continue their journey."

Since the early 1990s, people have enjoyed the water of Hoffman Spring under the Deer Park brand name.

Soldiers did pin strips of paper to their uniforms in some Civil War battles. Fletcher Pratt recorded this practice in his work *A Short History of the Civil War*. In the event the soldier was injured or killed in battle, the strip of paper would provide his identity.

The twin brothers and their best friend are fictional characters, but represent the divisions that occurred in the War Between the States, not only within the country, but also within families. Information about African Americans serving in the Civil War came from the book *From Slavery to Freedom* by John Hope Franklin. Franklin maintains that, by and large, white officers with some black noncommissioned officers led the African American troops.

Settlers

Set within the context of Oklahoma history, this is a true story of Doby Spring. Mr. Glen W. Crouch of Buffalo, Oklahoma, shared this story with the author who has retold it here. Mr. Crouch was very familiar with the spring. His father's homestead bordered the Doby ranch where the spring is located. Mr. Crouch is a local historian and a frequent presenter at the Harper County Conservation District Natural Resource Days.

Early explorers and the pioneers who settled this country often moved west from spring to precious spring. Stephen E. Ambrose notes in *Undaunted Courage* that Lewis and Clark marked springs as places for possible settlement.

President

Throughout time, people have visited springs for the purpose of restoring their health or energy. In some parts of the United States, Native Americans frequented springs for health and healing.

Depending upon the rock material through which it flows, spring water may contain different minerals. Eighteenth and nineteenth-century doctors had a limited number of medicines to prescribe to their patients. Therefore, they carefully recorded anything that seemed to work. One nineteenth-century doctor wrote a book about the mineral springs of Europe and the kinds of disease he thought each could treat.

However, belief in the health benefits of spring water was not limited to European springs. Americans also visited famous resorts in their own country to "take the waters." With the increase in population, the spread of industry and commerce, and the lack of knowledge about water resources, water quality in cities was becoming a concern. Also, because the cities were hot and uncomfortable in the summer, the wealthy liked to escape them for the season. A "spa culture" developed for social as well as health reasons.

Entrepreneurs built large hotels at the springs with such attractions as opera houses, tennis courts, golf courses, riding stables, bicycle and pony "tracks," and baseball diamonds where pro-league teams held their spring training. The hotels boasted accommodations for over 450 guests, elaborate ballrooms, and restaurants where exquisite meals were served. One young spa visitor wrote, "You have to change your gown or shirt every time you eat."

Famous people visited these spas: European royalty, movie stars, and American presidents such as William McKinley, Theodore Roosevelt, and William Howard Taft. Even Babe Ruth, the first great home run hitter in the history of baseball, "took the waters."

In the story "President," Danny and Liana are fictional characters, based on the personalities of real modern-day children. The setting for the story is the Spring House at the Poland Spring Resort in Maine. The author selected this spring house because its graceful and magical character hinted at stories to be told.

Danny and Liana's dog Turk is fictional, but Theodore Roosevelt actually mentioned a bloodhound called Turk in a letter to his daughter Little Ethel in January 1901.

Roosevelt's conversation with Danny and Liana is punctuated with many of the man's famous quotations. From the time he was a young man, Theodore Roosevelt was an avid believer in equal rights and equal pay for women.

Much of the background for the letter was gleaned from *Theodore Roosevelt, an Autobiography* and two biographies: *Theodore Roosevelt: A Life* by Nathan Miller, and *T. R.: The Last Romantic* by H. W. Brands. The story of young "Teedie" Roosevelt and the seal was true and did ignite Roosevelt's interest in the natural world. Believe it or not, the pony story is also true. It is recounted in *Theodore Roosevelt: A Life*.

Roosevelt's letters to his children are compiled in a volume entitled *Theodore Roosevelt's Letters to His Children* edited by Joseph Bucklin Bishop. They provide insight into the great man's love and sense of fun.

Language of Ground Water

Understanding how water moves under the ground and how springs are formed requires learning several new words. You could almost say it's like learning to speak "ground water." Remember, as with learning to speak any language, "practice makes perfect."

Aquifer – Ground water is often contained in an aquifer. An aquifer is an underground formation of saturated soil or rock that yields significant quantities of water that may be pumped to the surface for use by people, livestock, or watering crops.

Artesian Spring – A well or spring that taps ground water under pressure.

Atmospheric Water – Water in the gas, liquid, or solid state that is found in the atmosphere, such as water vapor, rain or snow.

Bedrock – A fairly solid mass of rock that makes up the crust of the earth.

Condensation – The process by which a vapor becomes a liquid; the opposite of evaporation.

Contaminant – Any substance that, when added to water (or other substances), makes it impure and unfit for consumption or use.

Down-gradient – The direction that ground water flows; similar to "downhill" or "downstream" for surface water.

Evaporation – The conversion of a liquid (e.g., water) into a vapor (a gaseous state), usually through the application of heat energy; the opposite of condensation.

Gravity – The natural force of attraction exerted by Earth on objects or materials on its surface that tends to draw them down toward its center.

Ground Water – Water found under the ground, either in the spaces between soil particles or in the pores, cracks, and fractures in rock material in the zone of saturation.

Hydrogeologist – A scientist who studies the geology of how water modifies Earth, especially through erosion and deposition, and ground water, with particular emphasis on the chemistry and movement of water.

Impermeable Layer – A layer of material (e.g., clay) that allows little or no water to pass through.

Percolate – The downward movement of water through layers of soil or other porous media.

Permeable Layer – A layer of porous material (rock, soil, unconsolidated sediment); through which water freely passes.

Pore Space – That portion of rock or soil not occupied by solid mineral matter and which may be occupied by water or air.

Potable – Water that is suitable for drinking.

Precipitation – Water falling in a liquid or solid state from the atmosphere to Earth (e.g., rain, snow, hail).

Recharge Area – The flow to ground water storage from precipitation, from streams, and from other sources of water.

Saturated – A condition in which all spaces between soil particles and in rock structures are filled with water.

Spring – A spring occurs where ground water naturally meets and emerges from the surface of the land.

Soil Moisture (Soil Water) – The water stored in soils that may either evaporate, be taken up by plant roots and eventually transpired, or that may continue to move down-gradient into ground water.

Surface Water – Water on the surface of the land, including lakes, rivers, streams, ponds, floodwater, and runoff.

Transpiration – The process by which water absorbed by plants (usually through the roots) evaporates into the atmosphere from the plant surface (principally from the leaves).

Unsaturated Zone – The area between the ground surface and the water table where the spaces among soil particles and in rock structures are filled with air and water. In the Saturated Zone every available space is filled with water.

Water Cycle – The paths water takes through its various states—vapor, liquid, and solid—as it moves throughout Earth's systems (oceans, atmosphere, ground water, streams, springs, etc.).

Water Table – This indicates the level below which soil and rock are saturated with water.

Well – A bored, drilled, or driven shaft, or a dug hole whose purpose is to reach underground water supplies or oil, or to store or bury fluids below ground.

Acknowledgements

The Watercourse appreciates the commitment of staff members who contributed to *Spring Waters, Gathering Places*.

Researcher: Kristen Limb

Reviewers: Dennis Nelson (Executive Director of The Watercourse and International Project WET), Bonnie Sachatello-Sawyer (Director of Education Projects), Linda Hveem (Executive Assistant), Gary Cook (WETnet Coordinator), John Etgen (Make a Splash Coordinator), Sally Unser (Administrative Assistant)

Production/Publishing Support: Chandra Morris (Publication and Production Coordinator), Stephanie Ouren (Operations Manager)

Thank you to Pete Schade, Geologist and the Montana Watercourse Volunteer Water Monitoring Coordinator, for reviewing "Spring Secrets" and the accompanying diagrams.

Thank you to Lee Esbenshade, editor and Ann Taylor, proof reader.

Thank you to Dr. Thomas McCoy, Vice-President of Research and Creative Activity, Montana State University for his commitment to The Watercourse and Project WET programs and publications.

In appreciation of the Project WET Coordinators who contributed in many ways to *Spring Waters, Gathering Places* including Don Hollums, Eileen Tramontana, and Hyder Houston who offered content suggestions.

A special thanks to Perrier Group of America for their support. To Kim Jeffery, Heidi Paul, and Kristen Tardif whose vision to provide education about water and springs for children, parents, and teachers was the inspiration for this publication.

The following Perrier staff members and associates reviewed the manuscript and provided their expertise: Kim Jeffery, Heidi Paul, Jane Lazgin, Marla Witteman, Ted Farthing, Jodie Adolfson, Madeleine Strass, Chris Berzolla, Jennifer Salera, Phillipe Riffi, Jeanette LaRock, Patrick Ford, Pamela Smith, Steve Abbott, and Andrea Schmauss.

Special recognition of the Perrier Geologists for their scientific review:
Rod Allen (Ice Mountain), Walter Anderson (consulting geologist, Poland Spring),
Meg Andronaco (Zephyrhills), Dave Feckley (Ozarka), Bruce Lauerman (Deer
Park), Dave Palais (Arrowhead and Calistoga), Kristin Tardif (Poland Spring)

Thank you to the following individuals:
Glenn Crouch for telling us his story about Doby Spring, Oklahoma
Tudi Feldman for information about Theodore Roosevelt
Patricia Flynn, Random House, Inc. for permission to print an adaptation of "The
Old Woman of the Spring" from the book *American Indian Myths and Legends* by
Richard Erdoes and Alphonso Ortiz
Otto Stein, Civil Engineer, Montana State University for his explanation of springs
Marie Watson for information about Arrowhead Springs
Amy Caso, teacher, for her review and suggestions

**With appreciation for the help of the Reference and Interlibrary Loan staff of the
Montana State University Library and the staff of the Bozeman Public Library.**

Thank you to the Theodore Roosevelt Association, Oyster Bay, New York